Orange Orangutan

Written by Mister Figg

Illustrated by Susan McClellan

Edited by Rita Fidler Dorn

This story is dedicated to all of you who are unique.

Special thanks to:
Darian and Heaven (my first two fans)
SFWA Novel/Short Story Critique Group

Created and printed in the United States of America

Miami, FL United States

One day when I arrived home from school, I saw in the empty lot behind my house, an orange orangutan who was dancing on a rainbow. Yes, it was dancing on a rainbow!

I asked it, "Why are you dancing on a rainbow?"

It answered, "I am looking for a fish to fly with."

I then asked, "Why do you want to find a fish to fly with? Wouldn't flying with a bird be easier?"

It answered, "You will find the answer by continuing your walk over there." The orangutan pointed to a mountain.

I walked and walked and walked...

...and I finally reached the mountain.

Then, I saw a polka-dotted porcupine!

It was swimming up the mountain! It was not swimming up a stream. It was swimming up the mountain!

I had so many more questions, so I walked up to the porcupine and asked, "Why do you have polka-dotted quills? How can you swim without water? Why are you swimming on land?"

It looked at me with a serious stare, and then responded, "I will answer your last question. I'm swimming up the mountain because I'm looking for a worm to jog with."

I became more confused. I replied, "Why are you looking for a worm to jog with? They don't have legs. Also, can you please answer my other questions?"

The porcupine then pointed to a clearing ahead of us as it said, "If you go over there, you will get your answers."

I walked to the clearing and saw many more things about which I had many more questions.

I saw all sorts of animals. I saw furry ones, scaly ones, feathery ones, ones with beaks, ones with lips, ones with snouts, and ones with noses. There were ones who swam, ones who flew. Ones who hopped, ones who crawled, ones who walked, and ones who slithered or slid.

They were different, but they were together. They were all doing strange things that I had never seen them do before. Nobody had seen them do these things before. You will have to use your imagination to picture all that I saw.

3/2019

I was going to start asking each of them questions, but a creature above me asked the most important question that I wanted to ask. "Why are all of these animals doing crazy things?" I looked up and saw that it was a ruby red raven.

Before I could ask the raven how it could be ruby red, and how could it talk, I heard a snort next to me.

I looked over and saw a raspberry and grape candy-horned unicorn! This unicorn seemed like it didn't like the questions. It said, "Don't ask questions. Just grab a gust of wind and join in by doing your own thing!"

As the unicorn trotted and the raven flew over to the other animals, I thought for awhile, and kept observing. Then, I finally figured out the answer.

It was that a whole bunch of animals were doing funny things...just to laugh and play and make friends.

I do have a question for you.

Do you want to be next doing something different, so you can play and make friends too?

Classic & Award Winners
Little Women
MADELINE
INTO THE JUNGLE
Curious George
Countdown
Treefrogs

About the Author

Mister Figg is a writer from South Florida. He was born in Brooklyn, NY and raised in Miami, Florida since he was about two years old. He is half Haitian and half Puerto Rican. Mister Figg mostly writes stories that take readers away from the everyday world. His goal is to always create a story that entertains and educates. Mister Figg is a former high school Language Arts and Journalism teacher in the Dade County Public School system. He has a BA in English/Literature from Florida International University. In his personal time, when Mister Figg isn't writing, he is a big fan of baseball and follows other sports. He is an independent member of the South Florida Writers Association.

About the Illustrator

Susan Massey McClellan is an artist from South Florida. She considers herself an "almost native" to South Florida, having moved to Plantation with her family at three and a half years of age from Baltimore, Maryland, where she was born. She has a Bachelor's in Design and Master's in Architecture from the University of Florida in Gainesville. Today, Susan is a practicing self-employed architect and interior designer in Fort Lauderdale. Her professional practice has always utilized her ability to draw visual glimpses for her clients, enabling them to also "see" a solution. Watercolor has been one of the mediums she continues to use in her practice. She has done numerous renderings for her clients' requests. Many of her historic preservation projects utilize watercolor renderings to enlist interest from outside sources. Her love of history and its details also has led her into drawing renderings for clients' books on local people and history. As a big believer in "giving back", Susan has volunteered on city advisory boards and committees, lending her professional expertise where it is requested.

About the Editor

Rita Fidler Dorn is a Native New Yorker, who grew up in Ohio, before she became a long-time Miami resident. Rita is a visible figure on the academic and creative scenes. She is a creator and facilitator of writing workshops for creativity, forgiveness, grief, and poetry construction. Rita is an English professor at Miami Dade College and Florida International University, and a former journalism teacher and news reporter. She has a BS in education from Ohio State University and MA in English from Florida International University. Rita is an independent member and serving Board Member of the South Florida Writers Association. Being a grammar guru and word game addict are among her personal joys. Her published books are Strands of Rhyme: Poems from the Real World (2014) and Poetry, My First Language (2018). Each volume: 91 poems about animals, nature, love, conflict, weather, colors, food, cities, and social commentary - serious and light, personal and global.

You can find out more about Mister Figg at

www.misterfigg.com

Twitter: @realMisterFigg

Instagram: @realMisterFigg

Mister Figg is an Independent Member of the South Florida Writers Association and the Society of Children's Book Writers and Illustrators.

www.southfloridawritersassn.org

www.scbwi.org

Made in the USA
Lexington, KY
30 October 2019

56284085R00019